Peppa Gives Thanks

Adapted by Meredith Rusu

This book is based on the TV series *Peppa Pig*. *Peppa Pig* is created by Neville Astley and Mark Baker.

Peppa Pig © Astley Baker Davies Ltd/Entertainment One UK Ltd 2003.

All rights reserved. Published by Scholastic Inc., *Publishers since 1920*. SCHOLASTIC

and associated logos are trademarks and/or registered trademarks of Scholastic Inc.

ISBN 978-1-338-22876-2

10 9 8 7 6 5 4 3 2 1
Printed in the U.S.A.

18 19 20 21 22
40

First printing 2018

Book design by Mercedes Padró

www.peppapig.com

SCHOLASTIC INC.

It is a lovely, sunny morning. Peppa and Suzy are having a tea party in the garden.
"I brought my teddy to join us!" says Peppa. "Did you bring your owl, Suzy?"

"No," says Suzy. "I brought my new Mr. Super Snuggles. He's the best bear in the whole world."

"What does he do?" Peppa asks.
"He can sing," says Suzy. "And say
'I love you.' And his eyes light up!"
"Wow!" says Peppa. "My teddy
can't do any of those things."

When Peppa gets home, she finds Mummy and Daddy Pig. "I would like a Mr. Super Snuggles, please!" she says.

"But you have a teddy bear, Peppa," says Mummy Pig.

"My teddy is *boring!*" Peppa snorts. "He can't sing or talk, and his eyes don't light up."

"Ho, ho, ho," Daddy Pig laughs. "Come, Peppa, let me show you something."

Daddy Pig shows Peppa a photo album.
There are lots of pictures inside.

"This is when we went camping," says Peppa.

"And to the beach..."

"And on a hot air balloon ride."

"And who is in all the pictures with you?" asks Daddy Pig.

"My teddy!" cries Peppa.

"Right," says Daddy Pig. "You've had Teddy ever since you were a little piggy. That makes him very special."

"We have to be thankful for the things
that we have," says Mummy Pig.
"What's 'thankful'?" asks Peppa.

"It means we're happy for the wonderful things in our lives," says Mummy Pig. "What are you thankful for, Peppa?"

Peppa thinks. "My toys!"
She runs upstairs. Her room is
filled with lots of lovely toys!
"What else?" asks Mummy Pig.

"Our house!" cries Peppa. "I love our house and our car and our garden!"

"Ho, ho," laughs Daddy Pig. "Anything else?"
"Hmm . . ." Peppa thinks.
"I know something I'm thankful for," says
Mummy Pig.

"What?" asks Peppa.
"You and George and Daddy Pig,
of course!" says Mummy Pig.
"Hee, hee, hee!" Peppa giggles.
"I'm thankful for that, too!"

"And I'm thankful for Suzy Sheep,
and all my friends," says Peppa.
"And Granny and Grandpa Pig!"

"Let's call Granny and Grandpa Pig right now," says Mummy Pig. "We can invite them to a special dinner."

Later that day, Granny and Grandpa Pig arrive.
Mummy and Daddy Pig make a delicious dinner for
everyone. Peppa and George help set the table.

"This looks wonderful!" says Granny Pig. "Thank
you for inviting us over."

"Peppa, would you like to tell Granny and
Grandpa what you learned today?" asks Daddy Pig.

"Yes!" says Peppa. "I learned that I'm thankful. I'm thankful for my toys and our house and my friends!"

"How lovely!" says Granny Pig.

"But most of all, I'm thankful for my family," says Peppa. "And my teddy."

Hee, hee, hee!
Peppa loves being thankful.
Everyone loves being thankful!
Especially when there's so
much to be thankful for.

This year, I am thankful for _____

_____

_____

_____

_____